THE ENGLISH UNDERSTAND WOOL

THE ENGLISH UNDERSTAND WOOL

HELEN DeWITT

STORYBOOK ND

Published by arrangement with the author

Manufactured in the United States of America
First published clothbound by New Directions in 2022

Library of Congress Cataloging-in-Publication Data
Names: DeWitt, Helen, 1957– author.
Title: The English understand wool / Helen DeWitt.
Description: First edition. | New York, NY : New Directions Books, 2022. |
Series: Storybook ND series
Identifiers: LCCN 2022005799 | ISBN 9780811230070 (clothbound ;
acid-free paper) | ISBN 9780811230087 (ebook)
Subjects: LCGFT: Novels.
Classification: LCC PS3554.E92945 E54 2022 | DDC 813/.54—dc23/
eng/20220204
LC record available at https://lccn.loc.gov/2022005799

10 9 8 7 6 5

New Directions Books are published for James Laughlin
by New Directions Publishing Corporation
80 Eighth Avenue, NY 10011

THE ENGLISH UNDERSTAND WOOL

1.

—The English understand wool.

My mother sat on a small sofa in our suite at Claridge's, from which the television had been removed at her request. She held in her lap a bolt of very beautiful handloomed tweed which she had brought back from the Outer Hebrides. She had in fact required only a few metres for a new suit.

I use the word "suit" because I am writing in English, but the French *tailleur*—she would naturally think of clothes in French—makes intelligible that one would travel from Marrakech to the Outer Hebrides to examine the work of a number of weavers, perhaps to establish a relationship with a weaver of real gifts. It makes intelligible that one would bring one's daughter, so that she might develop an eye for excellence in the fabric, know the marks of workmanship of real quality, observe how one develops an understanding with a craftsman of talent. The word "suit," I think, makes this look quite mad.

She had needed only a few metres, but she had bought the entire bolt to prevent it from falling into ignoble hands. We had stayed overnight on the way north in Inverness, where the shops were full of distinguished tweeds put to debased uses.

—*C'est curieux.* The Scots have the art, evidently,

of converting wool to this glorious stuff, but with this comes a genius for fabricating atrocious garments. One could not have imagined such monstrosities if one had not seen them.

She had returned to London to take the precious lengths to her tailor.

One would necessarily be in London for at least six weeks. Claridge's had installed, at her request, a Yamaha Clavinova with two sets of headphones in the space previously occupied by the television and the furniture which supported it. It would be mauvais ton to inflict one's music on persons who have expressed no desire to hear it (the Royal Suite and Prince Alexander Suite, each with its grand piano, surround the instrument with "buffer" rooms, but Maman had been unable to satisfy herself of vertical protection sufficient to shield a sensitive ear). It was a regrettable but necessary sacrifice to accommodate to the inevitable shortcomings of the digital instrument. One cannot, of course, dispense with a piano for more than a day or two; one gets out of the habit of practice with fatal ease. It is one thing to resign oneself in the Outer Hebrides, where arrangements are understandably primitive, but in the heart of London it would be absurd.

2.

The Irish understand linen the way the Scots understand wool. If one goes to Ireland for linen, which is, of course, unavoidable, one must avert one's eyes from the monstrosities perpetrated. (The excuse, if one ventures a remonstrance, is that the tourists like it.) Linen she did not have made up in London; she took it to a Thai seamstress in Paris. She had in fact accommodated the woman's desire to move to Paris from Bangkok; it is, after all, quite simple to make brief visits to Paris from Marrakech, whereas one cannot always go to Bangkok when one has had the idea for a frock, a redingote, a smoking.

The seamstress was equally gifted in cotton, silk, satin, velvet, brocade; only an imbecile would look to the English with such opportunities. Only an incurable optimist would look to a French modiste to realize one's fantasies; they follow the herd. One might see a redingote in *La Belle Assemblée* 1815, a caraco of 1787, a three-quarter-length coat in shantung with three-quarter-length sleeves from 1962; from the Thai seamstress one could commission something in the style and be enchanted with the result. In Paris only the darlings who run haute couture are permitted such flashes of inspiration; it's absurd.

Maman had advised prudence, the young woman

should establish herself in a provincial city, where rents were lower, and go to Paris when mastery of the language, a suitable accumulation of capital, permitted. (One could quite easily make quick visits to Marseille, Lyon, even Avignon.) The young woman said: Madame, I take pride in my art, I am happy to earn my bread in perfecting myself. But when I am not at work, I wish to be in Paris, where walking the streets makes one happy to be alive.

Surely this pride and this longing were inseparable from the genius the young woman had so often revealed? Maman had bought an atelier with a showroom in a useful arrondissement and placed it at her disposal.

It was understood that she would not fly in on a whim and expect the young woman to set all other clients aside; that would be mauvais ton. She expected only that appointments, once made, would be punctually observed. Anyone who has had dealings with the profession will understand that this is not a matter of small importance.

3.

The excursion to Scotland and then to London took place during Ramadan. It was her practice to spend Ramadan abroad, and to encourage my father to do so as well: Daddy always had any number of business trips on his plate, and there was no reason a sufficient number should not be lined up for the appropriate time. The servants remained on full pay. They might stay in the riad in Marrakech or visit their families, as they pleased. It would be mauvais ton to be waited upon by persons who were fasting. It would be mauvais ton to make the exigencies of religion an excuse to curtail their salaries.

The first time she did it she made a mistake. I was three years old when they bought the riad so I was too young to understand or remember, but she told me later that she had made a mistake, a gaffe. She came back the day after Eid. Imbecile. Of course they were all exhausted, both from the month of fasting and from the celebrations of the day before. It is good for one to be reminded of the depths of idiocy to which one can sink even when, or perhaps *particularly* when, one means well.

The following year she returned one week after Eid and was pleased with the results. The year after that she extended her absence, returning two weeks after Eid.

I do remember that year, because we spent six weeks

at a pony-trekking establishment in Wales. It was late in the year for pony trekking, and the owners were happy to receive the sort of consideration appropriate for six weeks, not only of mounting and lodging, but providing instruction for a five-year-old. In England, at any rate, it is important to ride as though one had been riding from the age of five, or rather it is important if one is invited to a country house, and the simplest method is, of course, to be taught to ride at the age of five. I was given my first riding boots, jodhpurs and hat, and when we returned to Marrakech Maman joined Les Cavaliers d'al-Hamra, a riding club (she had been backward, getting the house in order) so that I might have frequent opportunities to improve in this important skill.

It was, in fact, better to have six weeks at one's disposal. Maman liked to go to places where there are secret lives. Granada, Venice, even, yes, Paris—places where one can, of course, walk the public streets, the walls are high, barred, occasionally one catches a glimpse of a garden, or an open window at night, high above the street, spills golden light from a room lined with ancient volumes. (This is undoubtedly why she chose a residence in Marrakech.) Six weeks offer the courtesy of time. One will not be thrust in by chance invitations from the fool of the family, an impulsive youngster whose social blunders leave everyone rolling their eyes. There is the possibility of invitations of value. It is of no importance if these do not come; what matters is the glimpse of the garden, only to be entered by the favorites of chance.

She had left Eid gifts of 100 euros apiece for the staff,

and small gifts for the many children; the staff were, of course, on full pay for the additional two weeks. On her return the staff were full of energy, happy to execute the wishes of Madame. She declared her intention of making the six weeks' absence habitual henceforth.

4.

Maman was *exigeante*—there is no English word—in matters of protocol. Lunch, tea and dinner were served formally. English was spoken if my father was present, French if we were alone. It is important for the servants to become accustomed to the correct manner of serving; if the President of the Republic comes to dine, they must not be anxiously casting their minds back to the last important dinner. It is an advantage to them to speak both French and English flawlessly. (When they made mistakes, they were corrected.) If an opportunity arises in a great hotel, they will not be unprepared.

Maman spoke French with a pure Parisian accent. She used this in the normal management of the household; it was better for them to accustom themselves. She spoke the standard Arabic, the Arabic of television, of high-level functionaries, of international businessmen, on formal occasions where French was inappropriate. She spoke Darija, the Moroccan form of Arabic, when the servants were ill or had family problems. This was the hardest to learn because the language schools did not like to teach it, and private instructors felt they would lose face if they did not teach what was taught in schools. What she set out to do she did.

The servants did sometimes have the opportunity to work in grand hotels, but these did not offer six weeks at full pay for the month of Ramadan and a fortnight. They did not seize the career opportunity with alacrity.

On the contrary, my mother would find it necessary to sit down and explain the advantages. It was often she, indeed, who had put in the word of recommendation prompting the offer. Of course, she explained, perhaps there is not much to choose between serving in a household and waiting on tables, cleaning rooms, or even manning reception in a hotel, but in the latter there is the chance of advancement. If one is gifted and hardworking, one has the opportunity to rise—perhaps to the position of manager, perhaps even to owning a hotel. There are naturally many chances to meet persons of distinction. If one in fact prefers a domestic environment, one might enter the household of an ambassador, a member of the French nobility, an English gentleman. If one wishes to marry, to have a family, one cannot discount these things.

By the time I was seventeen perhaps twenty of our servants had passed on to employment in important households, in hotels not only in Marrakech but in Geneva, Venice, Granada, Paris, London, oh, a long list. There was naturally no difficulty in finding replacements for the household, or in firing these with enthusiasm for fulfilling the requirements of Madame.

5.

Hi Marguerite

Thanks for the pages, they definitely give a feel for what she was like and that's really helpful, but you don't say much about your feelings. She seems to have been quite cold, how did you feel about that? Were you hurt? Did you feel you had nowhere to turn? Did it ever occur to you, maybe just for a second before you told yourself it was crazy, that she was not actually your mother? Also, you don't say much about "Daddy," but this must have been quite a strange relationship. None of it could have happened without his technical savvy, he must be some kind of genius, but we don't get any sense of that, and we don't get any sense of why he didn't just take it all for himself. Just some thoughts, things to bear in mind as you go on.

Let me know if you'd like to rethink having a ghostwriter. I know you've been traumatized; when you've been through something like that sometimes it's easier to bottle it up inside, especially if you're working alone. Talking to someone might be an easier way to let it out, and then you can leave it to someone else to knock the text into shape, you can just get on with your life. I'm just putting this out there because at some point you're going to have to talk about the day you learned you'd been living a lie, and what they'd done to you. That's *going to be very hard. It might be easier to get through it if you just sat down and talked to someone for a day and then went out on the town!!!!*

xo

Bethany

Dear Bethany,

Thank you for your comments. I will bear them in mind. I think it is best for me to write what I know.

With regard to my father, I was told that he was an engineer. I did not know that he was a software engineer; this was not mentioned. In fact I think that he did start out with training in mechanical and electrical engineering. He took his first degree in 1983, which was, of course, before personal computers were widely available at a low price. He did not come from a comfortable background, so he did not have the advantages of, say, Bill Gates. Maybe when he came to programming it did feel like the Wild West, especially after the growth of the open source movement, but this is pure speculation.

My mother said that an engineer spent much of his time explaining things to people who were not engineers. It would not be amusing to be compelled to do this at the dinner table at the end of the day. We did not talk about his work because this would have been too much like the worst parts of his work. We talked about literature, philosophy, music, art. It is reasonable to suppose that this suited him, because if it did not he had no need to come home for dinner.

I will attempt to address the concerns you have raised.
With best wishes,
M/G

6.

Maman ordered a Pleyel from Paris because one wishes to play the pianoforte on the instrument preferred by Chopin. She was unable to find a sufficiently distinguished instructor in Marrakech.

She arranged for a gifted graduate of the Conservatoire to come from Paris for six months. The girl had completed her studies, but she did not wish to rush into the concert circuit, she wished to prepare a solid foundation for her programme. Maman bought a riad in the next street and installed a Steinway, which is regrettably necessary for the world of the concert. It was agreed that I would be permitted to sit in a separate room and listen to the hours of practice of this young musician for as many hours as I chose. If I wished to prepare a piece for her consideration I might do so. It was agreed that she would listen to any such piece at the end of a month. If the performance led her to believe that she would not find instruction intolerable, she would provide one hour's lesson a week. If she believed she would find instruction intolerable she was under no obligation to provide it; the riad was at her disposal for the full 6 months.

I was able to prepare three pieces to a standard which induced Mlle Sarian to provide weekly instruction for 5 months. It was necessary to practice four hours a day to continue to perform at a level which Mademoiselle would not find intolerable. I believe I was ten years old or thereabouts.

The arrangement made it straightforward to induce other gifted musicians to come to Marrakech on the same terms.

7.

Americans invented jazz; the French, Brazilians and Japanese also understand it. It is important to have formal training in the classical repertoire, but a true musician is not a train which can only run on the rails. My mother admired Bill Evans.

She bought a third riad and installed a sound studio. She arranged a room with an upright piano and space for other instruments. She persuaded a young jazz musician from Alaska to spend six months in Marrakech. If he did not find it intolerable he would introduce me to the mysteries of his art. He found it tolerable, and he was only the first.

8.

One must not expose adults to childish prattle. She in-
sisted that I should learn bridge at the age of seven
because one cannot always assume that a child can be
kept out of sight. By the age of ten my skills received no
compliments from her friends; they laughingly begged
to have me as partner—especially if there were to be
interesting stakes.

9.

It is important to play tennis. If one is invited to a château or country house one must not put one's hosts to the nuisance of arranging entertainment, one must be prepared to make up a party. It was straightforward to arrange lessons at the Royal Tennis Academy.

10.

Hi Marguerite

This seems like a lot of backstory, making the reader wait for the main event. If you don't talk about your feelings there is nothing to engage the reader and keep them turning the pages. I get the impression you're still bottling things up. Would it help if the two of us met and talked and I just recorded you on my cell to get it all down so there's something to work with? Or maybe you should skip ahead to the point when the truth came out?

Bethany

I did not know what to say so I did not reply.

I went to the Honors Club and found three bridge players looking for a fourth and my partner and I won $1,300. One of our opponents impulsively invited me to a house party at his place in Newport, where he said with a smile that they played games that were not quite so friendly. The other opponent invited me to a party at his apartment on Park Avenue in two days' time.

I was a little early, only half an hour after the stated time, because I was not sure how long it took to get places in New York. There was in fact a Steinway in the corner. The atmosphere was a little dry, I thought, with only a handful of people talking here and there; in the circumstances it did not seem to me to be mauvais ton to play, though no one had asked me to do so.

I played "Straight, No Chaser" and "Kind of Blue" and some other things. People came to the piano to talk and some brought me drinks and came back to talk some more. They knew who I was, of course. More people gave me invitations. I did not think they would have given me invitations if I had been talking about my feelings instead of dressing with éclat and playing bridge with flair and playing the piano when a party was off to a dull start. So perhaps there were people who would like to hear about feelings, but I did not think they were people I would want to know.

11.

Maman was to take the tweed to her tailor the day after we got to London. She had in fact also bought a bolt of a different tweed, not only because it must not fall into ignoble hands but because she thought I had stopped growing. That is, if she were to commission a *tailleur* for me there was a reasonable likelihood that I would continue to be able to wear it. It would be ludicrous if we had suits in the same fabric and wore them at the same time, and the fact that she had bought an entire bolt of one very beautiful tweed did not alter the matter, it had been necessary to buy a second. She thought that she might commission a riding jacket for me in the cloth being used for her suit.

We took possession of our suite around 4 p.m. Afternoon tea had been ordered in advance; it was brought just as we were arranging ourselves in the sitting room, enchanted by our return to civilization. We talked comfortably of one thing and another until it was time to change for dinner.

The telephone rang while I was showering.

We went to the restaurant. Maman was grave, looking over the wine list, but then it was her habit to be serious when ordering wine.

When the wine had come and the appetizers she began to talk a little.

The French understand wine, cheese, bread.

The Belgians understand chocolate.

The Italians understand coffee and ice cream.

The Germans understand precision, machines. (She in fact kept a Porsche in Paris.)

The Swiss understand discretion.

The Arabs understand honor, which embraces generosity and hospitality.

When I speak of these forms of understanding I do not mean that they are instantiated in every individual of a nation, a culture. I think of this thing which in France is taken so seriously, the terroir, the importance of a particular soil in conjunction with the water, the sun, the aspect of the land, and how this affects the grape. How this affects decisions concerning the grapes to be grown there. We see this likewise in the cheeses, the effect of the grass, the water, the breed of cow, on the milk and so on the sorts of cheese that are possible. It is as if certain qualities flourish in certain social conjunctions. Who can say why an English tailor knows what to do with Scottish tweed? If you explain yourself to him he will be able to understand.

So if you do business with an Arab, oh, of course, you can haggle over a brace of partridges in the street. But if it's a matter of importance, you might spend many hours drinking mint tea and talking of other things. You wait until each has decided whether he is dealing with someone he can trust. If there is no trust, there is no point in signing a piece of paper. This they understand.

If you deal with people who don't understand that, be very careful about what it says on a piece of paper.

I said that I would be careful. I asked if we might go riding in Hyde Park. I asked if it would be possible to play bridge at the Chelsea Bridge Club. I asked if we might hear Vengerov, who was playing at the Barbican. She said these things could certainly be arranged.

In the morning she was gone.

12.

It was quite common for me on our visits to London to rise early and breakfast alone in the dining room and walk in Green Park. I got back around 10 on this morning and found the door to her room open. A man in the hotel uniform was talking to a man in a tweed suit which showed little sign of the English genius for tailoring the material. This man introduced himself as Detective Inspector Braddock. I saw that my mother's suitcases were not on the suitcase rack; that the closet doors were open, the closets empty; that my mother was not in the room.

The detective asked if I knew where my mother might have gone. I said I did not. I asked if something was wrong. He said he needed to speak to my mother and any information I might give regarding her whereabouts would be helpful. For quite a long time he kept putting this question in different ways without explanation. I asked if I was under arrest. He laughed, a sudden bark of laughter, and seemed surprised at himself.

When it seemed to him that I either knew nothing or was declining to cooperate in my state of ignorance he did explain.

He said that I was an orphan. For one instant I thought that Maman and Daddy were dead, but he went on to explain that I had once been an orphan with a great deal of money. At the age of 20 months I had disappeared from the house of Bernard and Marie-Thérèse Dessanges, the guardians appointed in my parents' wills should both parents die while I was a minor, and a great deal of money left in trust for me, some 80 million euros (though it was not easy to be precise because some had been held in shares and some was in real estate and some was in accounts in different denominations) had also disappeared. The disappearance of the infant was, of course, the first circumstance to be discovered; the disappearance of the fortune came to light a few days later. At this point the disappearance of my birth father's personal assistant and technical advisor also came to light.

The Inspector passed over a photograph of a stout man of medium height with shaggy hair and a mustache disappearing in a full bristling beard. Daddy was clean-shaven, with short hair; he visited the barber once a week. He not only was but looked like someone who swam 50 lengths of an Olympic pool five days a week, played aggressive tennis on weekends in even the fiercest heat. These were undoubtedly incidentals, but I could not recognize him in this image of a slovenly ill-kempt nonentity. The Inspector passed over a photograph of a young woman whose close-cropped hair, whose unimaginative navy-blue suit and low-heeled shoes in the same color, gave an impression of undistinguished pragmatism. Maman was slim, elegant; she wore her gleaming blond hair sometimes in a chignon, sometimes loose, softly waved. Again, these were undoubtedly incidentals. The Inspector explained that papers relating to my identity had been found in the riad; DNA tests would be needed to confirm, but there was every reason to believe that I was the missing child.

There was, he said, some small amount of money, he could not say how much, which had not been taken. In due course I would presumably be assigned ownership of the riad and its contents. In the meantime, any information I could give leading to apprehension of the fugitives would naturally assist in recovery of my assets.

It was immediately obvious that there were perhaps hundreds of people who owed my mother a debt of gratitude, any of whom might well have assisted in her flight. Whether my father had a similar clientèle I did not know; it would not have been necessary.

It seemed to me that it would be mauvais ton to unleash the forces of the law on the Thai seamstress, or a young man working his way up through the ranks of a hotel in Geneva.

I was conscious, above all, of extreme anxiety not to be guilty of mauvais ton.

I was conscious of a slighter anxiety. It would not be possible for quite some time, perhaps years, to go to the Thai seamstress—I would inevitably be followed, and whether or not this led to the apprehension of the fugitives it would certainly cause chagrins. Where was I to find a seamstress?

13.

There was a matter of pressing concern. The servants expected to receive full pay in our absence. We had been away only ten days, and now there was no one to arrange for payment of these salaries. I called our housekeeper in Marrakech.

She did not burst into a flood of garrulous expostulation; she remained true to her excellent training. She assured me that funds for these salaries and the appropriate gifts had been left with her at the time of our departure. She added that a sum had been delivered to her in cash by private courier sufficient to cover expenses and salaries for an additional three months. The police, she said, had come with a warrant and removed papers. She had been given to understand that Monsieur and Madame would not be returning. She would await my instructions.

I expressed my gratitude. I asked her to convey my gratitude to the staff for their loyalty, upon which I should continue to depend.

14.

There was another matter of concern. Our appointment for an initial consultation with the tailor was at 3 o'clock. Not only could Maman not come for this appointment, the tweeds which were to form the basis of discussion had not yet been unpacked and were presumably still in one of her suitcases.

I called and explained that Maman had been called away on urgent business; it would be better if the consultation were deferred. I said it was my understanding that it was her custom to pay in advance and was assured that Madam had indeed paid for two ladies' suits and a riding jacket, fabric to be provided by Madam. It was the understanding of the tailor that Madam had made a special trip to the Hebrides to procure suitable fabric for the garments; it would be a pleasure to discuss this with Madam at her convenience. There was no awkwardness, though canceling at such short notice was what Maman particularly deplored; perhaps it was with a view to exceptional circumstances that she had made it her habit always to pay in advance.

It was suggested that I might like to come and have my measurements taken, on the understanding that work would proceed as soon as the desired fabric was available. I thought it would comfort me to spend an hour or two with a craftsman of talent; I gladly agreed.

15.

The affair was by no means leaked to the press. The police in London, Paris, and Marrakech held press conferences in an attempt to whip up media furore: someone, somewhere must have seen something. A reward was offered so that the investigation need not depend only on the strength of public spirit.

Journalists followed me in the street.

The bill at Claridge's had been paid in advance for six weeks. The management agreed to move me to a smaller suite, one with a single bedroom, removing the television and transferring the Yamaha Clavinova. I spent a week at the keyboard. It seemed to me that if I continued to work my way through Bach's *Well-Tempered Clavier* this would be a strong guard against acting in mauvais ton.

16.

I gave a number of interviews, not understanding that this would not put a stop to being followed in the street.

Messages were left by agents, lawyers, producers, publishers, and many others whose business was not specified.

The financial situation was complicated. It did seem as though if money could be obtained in some manner which did not involve unraveling this old fraud the situation would be simpler.

It was quite clear that any "biopic" would inevitably be in mauvais ton—one did not need Bach to see that! But a book, a text, this is something one can control.

I agreed to talk to several agents. There was no one with whom I would have chosen to do business, so, faute de mieux, I hired a man in New York with a reputation for getting impressive deals.

"Seven figures is definitely on the cards, but we need to get you to New York."

"Okay. I can be there in three days, I must have my hair cut. The appointment is made; it is naturally important to use a trusted stylist at this difficult time."

"Okay, okay, this could actually work to our advantage, give social media time to pick up momentum—"

"Can you make the arrangements? I shall need one first-class aisle seat on Air France—a genuine Air

France flight, not an American airline claiming to be Air France on the strength of a business partnership. And perhaps you could book me a suite at the Ritz. Ask them to remove the television and arrange for a Yamaha electronic piano in the Clavinova series, with headphones."

"Uh. I don't think the Ritz is a good idea, Marguerite. [The name of the infant was Marguerite; it was hard to get used to this.] Uh …"

"Is it not a good hotel anymore? The Four Seasons or the Mandarin Oriental would be perfectly acceptable, I leave it to your judgment."

"No, uh, at this point sympathy is key to the whole project, you have been robbed of one hundred million dollars by people who for reasons best known to themselves allowed you to believe they were your parents and abandoned you, leaving you penniless. Believe me, if you fly first-class and stay in a suite at a five-star hotel you're selling yourself short. You really don't want to do that. I know a great little B&B in Brooklyn, you'll love it. Taking the TV out, that works, it's too painful to be exposed to the media circus, people will understand. The piano, no. Not until a deal is in place."

This was execrable, but if one hires an agent it is surely stupid to ignore his advice, and perhaps it is also mauvais ton to imply contempt for his expertise. I agreed to fly economy class on Delta, United, or American Airlines; I agreed to a single room at this place in Brooklyn; I agreed to take the subway; I agreed to forgo a piano.

17.

The economy-class seat, the subway, the poorly staffed bed-and-breakfast in Brooklyn, these offered no protection of privacy, which perhaps was part of the plan. Not only were there journalists, there were members of the public taking photographs with their cellphones. An exclusive interview added fuel to this fire. Bert sent out a proposal to several publishers, an auction was soon underway, and within a week he had accepted an offer of $2.2 million for the North American rights. This was a triumph, because the publisher had naturally hoped to be given the world rights and been beaten down.

A contract was sent to me for approval. The contract of a minor must be cosigned by a guardian; there is no requirement for the guardian to engage in negotiations. Bert had stated his preference for dealing directly with the principal. The persons to whom the infant had been entrusted were happy to sign a document which removed any immediate need to provide financial support.

A contract was signed. A check for $1.1 million was sent to Bert. Bert's commission was $165,000. He had, it appeared, incurred expenses. A check for $915,000 was sent to me. At this point I had spent two weeks at the bed-and-breakfast in Brooklyn.

I deposited the check in an account opened for the

purpose and moved to a small suite at what was now, it seemed, called the Ritz-Carlton, from which the television had been removed and to which a Yamaha CLP-685 had been introduced. I proposed to write a first draft in one week and return to Marrakech. I had not anticipated the many objections raised by my editor to the sample pages submitted at her request.

18.

*Mais, quoique je veuille vous parler de la province pen-
dant deux cents pages, je n'aurai pas la barbarie de vous
faire subir la longueur et les* ménagements savants *d'un
dialogue de province.*

Stendhal, *Le Rouge et le Noir**

I am guilty of this barbarity. To recount what followed
is precisely to inflict on the reader the tedious machi-
nations of a dialogue de province. A hotshot publisher
or agent in New York does not feel like a provincial; the
tedium gives the game away. But one must be rational.

* I will not say that this is untranslatable; perhaps my English
is at fault. It easily escapes four professional translators, whose
attempts I offer below. The English reader is too often allowed
to believe that little is lost if French is left behind at school, or,
indeed, never studied at all.

> But though I want to talk to you about the provinces for two
> hundred pages, I lack the requisite barbarity to make you
> undergo the long-windedness and *circumlocutions* of a pro-
> vincial dialogue.   Horace B. Samuel, Heraklion Press, 1913

> But albeit I mean to talk to you of provincial life for two
> hundred pages, I shall not be so barbarous as to inflict upon
> you the tedium and all the clever turns of a provincial dia-
> logue.   C. K. Scott Moncrieff, Century Edition, 1926

If the object is not merely to entertain, but to instruct, those in need of instruction will feel the benefit. If some other young girl, with two million dollars at stake, finds this of use I shall count myself justified.

However, though I fully intend to talk to you about the provinces for a couple of hundred pages, I haven't the heart to subject you to the tedium and *astute manoeuvring* of a provincial conversation.   Roger Gard, Penguin Classics, 2002

But though I propose to tell you about provincial life for some hundreds of pages, I will not barbarously submit you to the prolixity, the *wise heavy-footedness* of country conversation.   Burton Raffel, Modern Library, 2003

19.

Hi Marguerite

We need to talk. I've made reservations for lunch to-morrow at Le Pain Quotidien around the corner from the office. The afternoon is booked solid with meetings I can't reschedule at short notice, so please come promptly at 1.

Best

Bethany

20.

New Yorkers are extraordinary. One has a business matter of some delicacy to discuss, a personal matter so fraught it cannot be resolved over the telephone, and the New Yorker's immediate instinct is to arrange a meeting in a crowded place where anyone might over-hear. One proposes meeting in a hotel room, a private office, the home of the person concerned, and this is met with deep suspicion, not to say revulsion. The number of restaurants in New York ensures that one could always be sure of privacy in some struggling establishment, but no, the instinct is to thrash things out in a popular venue at *the height of its traffic*.

It seemed to me that a compromise was in order. I would not insist on a private meeting, but I would propose a venue where we need concern ourselves only with the discretion of the waiters.

21.

Dear Bethany

I am happy to meet you tomorrow for lunch. In view of the urgency implied by your e-mail, I assume you have serious concerns about the direction of the book. I suggest that we meet at Deux hommes dans Manhattan, whose excellent food has yet to win it a following. If you can meet me at 1 we can regrettably be certain of being alone.

With best wishes,
M/G

Marguerite

Fine. See you there.
B

22.

I wore a pale salmon shift in twilled silk, a simple string
of pearls, pearl earrings, and deep salmon half-d'Orsays
of Italian leather with a modest 3-inch heel. I was punc-
tual to the appointment in view of Bethany's heavy com-
mitments in the afternoon.

When she had not come in ten minutes I placed an
order, bearing in mind the preferences shown at the tri-
umphal dinner celebrating her success in the auction.
One could at least ensure that no inroads were made
into the time on which such heavy claims were made.
The wine list was not contemptible; I ordered a bottle
of the Puligny-Montrachet (it seemed courteous to accommodate someone whose tastes ran to white).

She came rushing in at 1:15. She wore white patent-
leather shoes; these distracted me from the muddle of
garments thrown together seemingly at random. (It
seemed unkind to condemn these; New York offers hid-
eous garments in an abundance rivaled only by Scotland. The shoes were inexplicable.) She sat down; I was
able, with some difficulty, to take my mind off the mys-
tery of the shoes.

"I have put in the order," I said, "as I understand you
are pressed for time. I thought you might like the *tartare
de crevettes à la citronnelle gingembre et caviar*, and the
grilled wild salmon with chanterelles, pan-softened heir-

loom tomatoes and wild rice. The Puligny-Montrachet will, I think, be in harmony, and it is an excellent year. Now that you are here you can naturally, if you wish, order the dessert you prefer."

I had already tasted and approved the wine; if it had been unacceptable a replacement could have been ordered without loss of time to the businesswoman. I hoped she would understand that the glass of wine at my place was not a mark of bad manners but of thoughtfulness.

"But—" Bethany had dropped a bulging handbag to the floor and was staring at the glass.

I said hastily, "This is on me. These people in accounts, it's their job to question expenses, you can't expect them to understand the importance of good wine. You don't want to get into that argument."

"Yeah, but—Thanks, Marguerite, but, um, you're *seventeen*. It's not legal for you to drink alcohol until you're twenty-one. I mean, it's not legal for them to serve you. I don't understand, how did you get them to let you get away with that?"

This was precisely the sort of idiocy one would expect from someone who wore white patent-leather shoes.

"I asked for the wine list. I placed an order. If you tell me this is illegal, well, we are in the realm of speculation. Maybe they respect someone who respects good wine. Maybe they're tired of people who come and order the cheapest thing on the list, or order whatever they happen to sell by the glass. Maybe they think the law is stupid if it criminalizes a seventeen-year-old who understands wine. Or maybe the waiter wants a big tip from the only customers to walk in at lunchtime. Or maybe they just had a raid and don't expect another. Or maybe they have a deal with the police. Or maybe they think the table can't be seen from the street. Surely this is not what you wanted to discuss."

"No, no, it's just that, but okay, never mind." The waiter had appeared at her elbow to fill her glass. "I shouldn't," she said, "but oh, God." She sipped once, again, sighed. "Well, you sure know how to pick 'em."

"I'm glad you approve," I said.

She took another sip. The waiter slid appetizers in front of us and withdrew.

"Okay," she said. "Look. Marguerite. I understand. This is the only family you knew. Suddenly you're alone in the world; you've always been alone in the world. It's hard to take it all in. But masking your emotions doesn't work for a book, it really doesn't. Normally, you could take as much time as you needed to process. A book has a timetable, a publication date. You can't necessarily take the time you would like to take. I know that's hard, but in the long term, you've been given financial security, once the book is out there you can have as much time as you need to adjust. In the short term, we really need a book that will work."

I said, "I understand that the book needs to work."

"Let me ask you again. Did it really never strike you that the woman you thought was your mother was cold? She comes across as very cold."

I said, "No."

"Maybe you were conditioned not to recognize it because you'd never known anything different. You don't
talk about your feelings. You come across as cold. I tell
you that and it's as if you don't know what I'm talking
about. How did you feel when you learned she was not
your mother?"

I said, "If you look at photographs—"

I said, "I accept that the woman in the early photographs with the infant was my biological mother. At the
time of her death, I am told, I was 18 months old. It goes
without saying, I could not have made an intelligent
choice of guardian at 18 months. Maman gave me the
chance, many chances to show I was not a mediocrity,
and in this way I earned the right to participate in the
life bought with this money by a person of distinction. If
I had not done so, she would not have been ungenerous;
she would have made provision in accordance with my
capacity."

Bethany was not eating her appetizer. The waiter
came to take my plate. I said, "Shall we let him bring
the entrée? It will destroy the flavor if it sits in the
kitchen."

She said, "Oh, sure. Sure. But. Marguerite. When you
talk about earning the right. It was yours. She, they,
you—you don't understand. We're talking about One.
Hundred. Million. Dollars."

I said, "I understand that one hundred million dollars is a great deal of money, and today, at seventeen,
with my training, I could make intelligent use of one
hundred million dollars. But at 18 months I could not

have used this one hundred million dollars to arrange to be brought up by the equal of Maman. No doubt she has her equals, but at 18 months I could not have found them. At four years, five, six, I could not have done so. At ten I could not have done so. I might have remained in possession of this one hundred million dollars and lost fifteen years I could not get back again. Now, of course, I do not have one hundred million dollars, but I have 2.2 million dollars minus Bert's commission and I have the riad and I do not understand this grievance you expect me to feel."

There was a little silence. There was a little indrawn breath. She had finished her first glass of wine and the waiter had refilled the glass and now she took three gulps, which was not what the wine deserved.

"Marguerite," she said at last. "There's this thing called the Stockholm Syndrome, which—"

I said, "Of course I know the Stockholm Syndrome."

She said, "So I understand. I understand. But I have to tell you that you do not in fact have two million dollars, give or take. You have been paid $1.1 million upon signature, the remainder to be paid upon delivery of a manuscript which is satisfactory to the publisher. Normally the payments would be made in three tranches, the third upon publication; one of the key points in the auction was that preference would be given to a publisher who paid in two tranches, upon signature and upon delivery. We believed in the book, so we went for it. The contract was quite specific about the areas we would expect to see covered; this is normal when the value of the book to the publisher hinges on topics of particular media interest. In the event that the manuscript is not satisfactory, the second tranche will not be paid. In the event that you make no reasonable attempt to meet our requirements, not only will the remainder not be paid, but you will be required to return the initial advance. I have to remind you, in case Bert did not make this clear: on the very rare occasions when an author does this, the agent keeps his commission. He did his job by selling the book; if the author is not willing to fulfill his or her part of the bargain, there is no reason for the agent to be penalized. So if you are not able to make a real effort to meet me halfway you would need not only to return what you were paid, but also to make up Bert's commission. I suggest you talk to your agent and lawyer before making a final decision."

I said, "Certainly I will talk to them. But are you really not going to eat your lunch? Mine is very good."

She cut a piece from her fish and put it in her mouth. (The heirloom tomatoes remained unhappily to one side, the wild rice and chanterelles now mournfully sodden in the watery juice.)

She chewed and swallowed.

She said, "I know what you've been through. But this is a business transaction; there's nothing I can do."

I said, "I understand that it is a business transaction, Bethany. Look, I know it's rude, but would you mind if I called Bert now? You might be more comfortable if everything was settled."

"If you want to be private I can go the Ladies or

something."

"No, no, it's fine," I said. "I just want to be sure I understand the legal situation."

I took out my cellphone. I had never used a cellphone in a restaurant, but we were still the only customers, so perhaps it was acceptable in view of Bethany's distress. I called Bert's cellphone, since he too would naturally also be at lunch. He took the call, so it was probably not an important lunch. He confirmed the legal provisions as outlined by Bethany and confirmed also that, if I was unable to work constructively with my editor to the point where it was necessary to return the advance, his commission would not be similarly refundable. I thanked him for clarifying the matter and called my lawyer.

I had hired the lawyer because I did not know Bert. It seemed useful to have an independent review of legal documents negotiated by the agency.

My lawyer was also, naturally, at lunch, but he too took the call. He confirmed that this was the force of the contract, whose terms were standard for this kind of deal. I thanked him for clarifying the matter.

Bethany had been making good progress with her lunch. I had not become distraught; I had not burst into tears, or hurled recriminations. It was reasonable to suppose that I understood that this was a business transaction.

I returned my cellphone to my bag.

"Bert and Larry have confirmed your account of the contract," I said.

"I'm sorry, Marguerite, but it's pretty standard for this kind of deal; when people take that kind of money they go into it with their eyes open. If Bert didn't make that clear to you he wasn't doing his job, but you'll appreciate, we have that clause there for a reason, if there's a clear contractual violation I can't just let that slide."

"I understand that," I said. "Do you have a copy of the contract with you?"

"No, but I can have our contracts guy e-mail it over if you need to check something."

I said, "No, I have it here. I suggest you read it. I don't think the contract says what you think it says."

I took the document from my bag and placed it on the table by her plate.

23.

Bert had sent me the contract in a Word document attached to an e-mail. He drew attention to the fact that the advance was for North American rights only, and also to the fact that it would be paid in two tranches. He assured me that the terms were the best possible terms. I should read it and if it was acceptable to me I should print out five copies, sign them, and overnight the signed copies to the Dessanges for signature and overnight return. If there was something I had a problem with we could definitely discuss it but it was a good contract, everyone was enthusiastic about the project, and the sooner we got the contract back to them the sooner I would have money to see me through this difficult time.

I read the contract and was surprised.

When a film contract is negotiated, there is often a clause specifying the amount of nudity which may be required of the actor. It's understandable that it might be harder to achieve this level of specificity in a book contract: it is easy to determine whether a breast is clothed or bare, and not so easy to determine whether a metaphorical breast has been bared. So maybe you can understand why there is a clause about what is acceptable to the publisher that is really only vaguely specific. But in that case, maybe someone decides that the fantasies you used when masturbating reveal your feelings about your mother, and there must have been such fantasies and they must go in the book, and according to the contract if you don't even try to do this you must give back all the money. You are being asked to sign when you don't know what you are agreeing to.

If you were dealing with people of similar background you would know. But if you are dealing with people who are blind to bad taste there is no way of knowing.

So I amended the contract to give the editor the right of consultation. A manuscript would be deemed acceptable if covering the facts, including those relating to alleged embezzlement by and disappearance of the supposed parents, to the extent that these were known to the author. Such facts would include the author's response to the extent that the author thought necessary. No changes could be made to the manuscript without the author's approval. In the event that the publisher chose not to publish the book the remainder of the advance would still be payable.

I was surprised that the contract had not been sent in a watermarked PDF, for example, but no doubt all concerned were anxious to close the deal while the author was isolated, distraught.

I printed five copies in the office of the bed-and-breakfast. I signed them. The bed-and-breakfast was not in the habit of organizing FedEx collections for its guests, but the owner was eager to help; I sent the documents to the Dessanges, explaining that they must sign the papers and return them to Bert. Bert sent the documents to the publisher's lawyer. The publisher's lawyer sent the documents to Bethany, who signed them and returned three copies to Bert; one was returned to me and one sent to the Dessanges. The check was sent, of course, to Bert.

24.

Bad masters breed bad servants. If one is seventeen and inexperienced, one is reliant on persons whose integrity and competence cannot normally be verified. So perhaps it is irregular for the author to amend a contract that has been negotiated, but a seventeen-year-old might not know this and one would expect an experienced agent and lawyer to check. One would expect the editor and publisher's lawyer also to check, because otherwise they are relying on the author's agent and lawyer to protect them from the inexperience of the author.

It was useful to know that none of these persons had bothered to check. They relied, it seemed, on the inexperience, the financial weakness, the presumed emotional fragility of the author to push through a contract which stood to her disadvantage, but they did not anticipate the operation of these factors as perhaps suggesting terms she might prefer.

25.

Bethany was opening and closing her mouth like a goldfish.

She said, "Where did you get this? I don't understand."

I said, "Bert sent it to me the day you signed it. If you look at your copy you will see it says the same thing."

She said, "But this is not what was agreed."

I said, "Bert sent me a Word document as an attachment. He told me to sign it and send it to my guardians and have it signed and returned if it was acceptable. I sent them a document that was acceptable to me. If it was not acceptable to you, it would have been better not to sign it."

Bethany opened her mouth and shut it and opened it again. She said, "Marguerite. Do you mean to say that you *doctored* the *contract*?"

"I amended the language to avoid ambiguity," I said.

"But you just can't—you can't do that. You don't understand. Publishing is a business that depends on trust. I would *never* have signed something like—"

"I am only seventeen," I said. "I thought people did not sign contracts they had not read, when important sums of money were involved. In these days of electronic transmission, it is so easy for the wrong document to be attached; so easy for changes to be agreed and made and the revised file not saved. One would not expect a seventeen-year-old girl who had been through recent emotional trauma to catch such errors."

"That's complete and utter bullshit. You knew—"

"You speak of the importance of trust," I said. "The document I was sent did indeed require a heavy investment of trust on my part in persons I barely knew. A seventeen-year-old girl who has just suffered what is, in your view, the greatest betrayal imaginable from those to whom she was closest could not be expected to place this level of trust in perfect strangers."

"I keep forgetting," said Bethany. "Dear God, I keep forgetting. You were raised by crooks. You were raised by people who pulled off the heist of the century. I can talk till I'm blue in the face. You just don't get it."

She pushed back her chair and stood up. "I strongly doubt the validity of this document. Until I have ascertained that, there is no point to further discussion. I will talk to our lawyer; he will, no doubt, be in touch with your agent."

I stood up out of courtesy. I said, "Bethany, by all means, talk to a lawyer. But once you talk to your house lawyer—look, he sent it to you but he didn't *sign* it, his name isn't on the contract, and once you talk to him you have no control, because he is not answerable to you, he is answerable to the company. If you will take my advice, you will retain an entertainment lawyer and talk to him first, because then you are the client, and if you want it to go no further it will stop. Because maybe the book you will get is not the book you wanted, maybe it is not a book you want to pay another million dollars for, but nobody knows what happened unless you tell them. Whereas if you go to litigation to recover what you already paid, you can only recover what's left after legal fees, unless you try to force me to sell the riad, at that point maybe the story is worth a lot to some other publisher. But even if you don't go to court it doesn't help, because I go to court to get the million dollars you still owe me, and I have about $900,000 to fight the case so maybe I could win it and get costs. Of course, don't trust this as legal advice, because I'm not a lawyer, but talk to your own counsel first."

"Screw you," said Bethany. She picked up her big clumsy bag and stalked out to the street.

26.

Protocol dictates that one should speak first to one's agent. This had not been possible since I had been in the middle of an editorial lunch.

I summoned the waiter and ordered a crème brûlée, a double espresso and a cognac. The waiter wrote this down with aplomb, showing no gêne at the underage request for a cognac.

I took out my cellphone. I was still the only customer in the restaurant, so perhaps it was acceptable.

Bert would naturally still be at lunch. I did not want to interrupt his lunch for the second time with unpleasant news; I called the office and left a message, explaining that the terms of the contract had been unfamiliar to the editor and she was unhappy with the situation.

I left a similar message for my lawyer, seeing no reason to interrupt his lunch with unpleasant news.

I ate my crème brûlée with an enjoyment unalloyed by the dismal spectacle of Bethany's monstrous ensemble. The espresso was a joy, the cognac a very great pleasure.

I was not confident of having entirely avoided mauvais ton in the discussion. I had refrained from a very large number of unflattering comments; it seemed to me that I had not done badly in the circumstances.

If the person in Bethany's job had not been a mediocrity, she would not have found herself so awkwardly placed. She would, in the first instance, not have signed a contract of this importance without reading it. But no, that is really in the last instance. In the first instance, she would have invited the traumatized victim of betrayal and abandonment into her home. She would not have bleated of feelings as a way to sell a book, or cast around for some flunkey paid to elicit such feelings in a fake heart-to-heart. She would have talked quietly and pleasantly late into the night, permitting expression of whatever the guest chose to express. She would not have allowed a lawyer to go in and do her dirty work, putting clauses in place to coerce confession while she modestly averted her eyes—only to come out waving a stick when things did not go her way.

Of all this I had said nothing. This at least was very much to my credit.

27.

I took the subway to Battery Park and boarded the Staten Island Ferry. It was sparsely populated at this time of day, about half past two. Halfway to Staten Island my cellphone rang.

It was Bert. He was extremely angry. Bethany had in fact called him on his cellphone rather than waiting to talk to a lawyer. He had returned to his office after an abbreviated lunch and examined the contract. He said the relationship was one of trust, if there wasn't trust it wouldn't work.

I said, "I see that I have violated some sort of etiquette, Bert, but look. We now know that the contract you negotiated was a bad one, because the editor was going to use it to force me to tell a lot of lies, and if I did not want to tell a lot of lies I would not only have to give back the money but sell or mortgage my riad, the only asset currently at my disposal, to cover your commission for negotiating a bad contract. I am only seventeen, but I know that one does not hire an agent to be compelled to sell or mortgage one's assets to cover the compensation he has received for enabling an editor to force one to sell or mortgage one's assets."

Bert said that he had to work with these people. He said that Bethany was the best in the business, she had the savvy to make the book a $2.2 million book, and if I was not willing to make use of this savvy the value of the foreign rights would drop right through the floor.

28.

I disembarked at Staten Island. There appeared to be nothing of interest in the immediate vicinity of the terminal. I joined a queue for the return and was presently borne in the direction of Manhattan.

My cellphone rang. My lawyer was also very angry.

If my lawyer, or a member of his staff, had compared the signed document with the e-mail attachment, he might have drawn this to the attention of Bert. Bert had lost face, and the lawyer had lost face by permitting Bert to lose face. That is to say, he might have called Bert and said that he was in agreement with the amendments introduced to the document; while appearing to uphold the interests of his client he would in fact have been calling the changes to the attention of one who would in a similar fashion have drawn them to the attention of the publisher in a manner designed to deny responsibility.

It seemed to me that a lawyer who did not review a document to which changes might have been made must be of a singularly trusting disposition.

29.

Bethany had a conversation with Bert, the gist of which was that the delivery date was in six months, a period of time which might allow me to get in touch with my feelings. Regardless of when I submitted the text, she would like to allow this time to pass before making a decision—particularly as it was possible that, if the fugitives were caught, this would add to the interest of the story and also, perhaps, allow me to stop bottling up my feelings.

I pointed out that the contract required the publisher to pay the second tranche within one month of delivery of a manuscript deemed acceptable, and did not specify a date before which a submission could not be made.

Bert strongly advised giving the editor this flexibility. I took this to mean that six months would give her time to look for another job. If a new editor were responsible for taking delivery of the manuscript, the publisher would no doubt be legally required to pay for it, but it would not be the editor's responsibility. Bethany's new employer would be unlikely to fire an employee for an imprudent deal struck at another company.

I agreed to this in principle, specifying only that, if Bethany were to find another job in the interim, I should be at liberty to submit the book immediately upon her departure.

30.

A friendly e-mail from Bethany laid much weight on the interest which would be added to the narrative if the fugitives were apprehended.

31.

Maman had once shown me a handsome burqua grilla-gée which she had bought when the Moroccan govern-ment closed down their manufacture and sale. It was deep blue and had the very fine pleats one associates with Issey Miyake. She had bought ten, she said, some jet black, some in the range of blues (blue is typical of Afghanistan, black of Saudi Arabia): the government had ordered all stock to be liquidated within 48 hours, and she did not like to see so excellent a craftsman exposed to unmerited financial difficulties. Perhaps I looked surprised. She said that one could not know how one's circumstances might change. The press is intru-sive these days; one might need to take special mea-sures to ensure one's privacy in the street.

She had for many years had a collection of chadors, some of silk and wool, some of silk and cotton, in ivory, black, tobacco brown, maroon; one could not know where one would travel, and it might be convenient to change one's style of dress in conservative districts.

I reflected that my father was in fact shorter in stat-ure than my mother. Garbed in a burqua or chador, he might without difficulty pass for a woman.

I contemplated Maman going to a man who had been unable to pay for his daughter's wedding. I contem-plated Maman going to a woman whose son now owned a fleet of taxis. I contemplated the fact that she had the jewels. I contemplated rising young men in hotels the length and breadth of Europe who owed their position to her good offices.

I could not envisage this capture which was to enliven the narrative.

It seemed tactful to permit Bethany to conduct her job hunt unremarked.

32.

I have omitted to mention one circumstance.

It is true that on the day of the disappearance Maman's suitcases were not on the rack and the closets were empty. In my own closet I later found a three-quarter-length coat with three-quarter-length sleeves in pistachio shantung—pistachio being, of course, one of the few colors which can be worn by a blonde and also by one with chestnut hair. Maman was 6 centimetres taller than I was; it was naturally necessary for the garment to be adapted to one of my height.

I had hesitated to approach the Thai seamstress, but I now saw that I had been foolish; I had been imagining that Maman had been stupid. There was no need to know the precise details of her transactions with the seamstress. Perhaps the property was already in the young woman's name, perhaps it was in the name of a corporate entity in whose documentation Maman's name did not appear; whatever prudence would have dictated would have been done. Those who understand clothes might understand the importance of the relationship, but the investigators had shown themselves to be wholly oblivious to matters of taste; it would not occur to them that a seamstress might be a significant contact.

I called Paris to explain my requirements and was

told I could have an appointment in two weeks' time.

I told Bethany I must go to Paris for one week.

"Whatever."

I booked a return ticket on Air France for a first-class seat on the aisle. I booked a suite for one week at the Hotel Charles de Gaulle. I flew to Paris and presently walked into the little showroom and was taken upstairs to the atelier.

Mlle Srisati took me into her office. She expressed her pleasure in seeing me again. She said that she could easily adapt the coat in two days. She asked me to dress myself in the coat; she made notes on a small pad. She pinned the hem and cuffs of the sleeves. She placed her hands on the shoulders and said it would be necessary in fact to take these in for a narrower frame.

She said, "Oh! Madame has left you a parcel."

She took a brown-paper parcel from a drawer and placed it in my hands.

I returned to the Hotel Charles de Gaulle and unwrapped this parcel.

Within were two smaller parcels.

In one, a narrow box containing a rope of pearls, a pearl and diamond brooch, pearl and diamond earrings. A note: These were among the effects of Mme Despinasse. One sees that she was not invariably devoid of taste.

In the second, a bolt of very beautiful handloomed tweed. A note: Take this to Peter Craven of 34, Savile Row. The English understand wool.

AUTHOR'S NOTE

In the Renaissance blue was an expensive pigment; a patron commissioning a painting would specify how much blue the painter was to use. Today we have new possibilities and new sources of prohibitive expense

In 1983 Edward Tufte took out a second mortgage on his house to self-publish the first of a series of spectacularly handsome, fiercely uncompromising books on information design. Self-funded, he could bring in a first-class book designer, Howard Gralla, for an entire summer of collaboration. Tufte's unsuspecting readers would presently find that books of an apparently technical nature had the capacity to excite rage, delight, pity, contempt, ecstasy, even visceral horror at objects formerly seen with at most tepid interest (charts, signs, maps, diagrams, timetables, the ubiquitous PowerPoint).

The books are now classics, but the power of their principles has yet to be put at the service of fiction.

A writer without Tufte's resources must do a great deal independently (it's not uncommon for hours of coding, of refining results in design software, to produce a single image within a text).

Readers have been extraordinarily generous in helping me, with everything from the replacement of a laptop to a subscription to Adobe Illustrator to offers of tech support (and more, too much more to list here). If you'd like to support new work or just buy me a coffee, you can do so on my blog (paperpools.blogspot.com) or at at ko-fi.com/dewitt.

HELEN DeWITT